I0788367

# Princess Slutty-Pants

by Janine Jeffreys

Illustrations by Marisa Martin

Dedicated to all the girls who
have lost their pants.

It's ok.

Once upon a time, there was a very happy and successful couple, Harry and Louisa. They had everything that any happy and successful couple could possibly want. They had a beautiful house, sleek cars, travel to exotic destinations, everything in fact with the exception of just one thing, a child. At first, when no child appeared, Louisa was a little sad because producing a child was something that all her friends seemed able to do with a minimum of effort. Harry didn't really mind. Babies are messy and very very needy, and while he wanted Louisa to be happy, he didn't really want to be up all night with the crying and the feeding and the thought of his beautiful, elegant wife in vomit covered sweat pants was truly upsetting. But as it happened they built a very agreeable life together. Attending parties, dinners at all the best restaurants, flying to all corners of the world at a moments notice. And babies became the very last thing on their minds, that is until, until she was there, a very real, very beautiful, baby girl. It was a shock, well, a surprise, like a party where everyone hides in the dark and then shouts "SURPRISE!" as the lights blind you and your heart almost jumps out of your chest and your stomach turns summersaults. But it would only be a very rude person who would cry, "I don't want a fucking surprise party! Fuck off the lot of you and go home!" Louisa and Harry were not rude people.

So, they called their perfectly beautiful daughter Princess because she was special and would be given all the very best things that a little girl could possibly want. Because Princess was definitely going to be the only little girl they would ever have (no more surprises) they decided to give her some extra special names: one from each of them. They thought of the things they loved the most. Louisa chose Summer because that was the time of year when it was warm and they flew to far off tropical islands and sipped exotic cocktails and charming men admired her and Harry didn't have to work in the summer, because he'd already made lots of money, and he admired her too. Harry chose Pie because when he held the perfect pink bundle in his arms the sweet baby smell was so comforting and warm it made him remember when he was a young boy and his mother would bake the most marvellous pies with pastry so buttery and fillings so delicious. She smelt like love.

Louisa was a great beauty, with wit and charm in abundance. Harry was a big man with a big personality and a big appetite for all the things the world had to offer, and not just pie. Princess Summer Pie was a perfect combination of the two. She was happy and healthy and no trouble at all. She caused barely a blip to her parents' lifestyle and the home help adored her. Of course her parents adored her too, just not as often.

SURPRISE!

By the time Princess Summer Pie was 29 she had learned a few things:

1. Princess Summer Pie was not the best name in the world. Children laughed at her and adults rolled their eyes. She was not a princess. Summer was hot and lonely. Pie was a soft, gooey, microwaved thing that made ice cream melt too fast. She called herself PSP.

2. Being adored for being beautiful was not all it was cracked up to be. She had trouble keeping girl friends because their boyfriends liked her way too much. And even though she never had any trouble finding male company she very often felt that they didn't "get" her. They saw her as a prize rather than the strange, clever and wonderful girl she was.

3. Lately, her friends had taken to calling her Princess Slutty Pants and that was just fine. If there was one thing PSP was proud of, it was her exquisite, hand made and designed by herself, pants. And maybe many people saw those pants but really they were just too wonderful to be kept locked up at home.

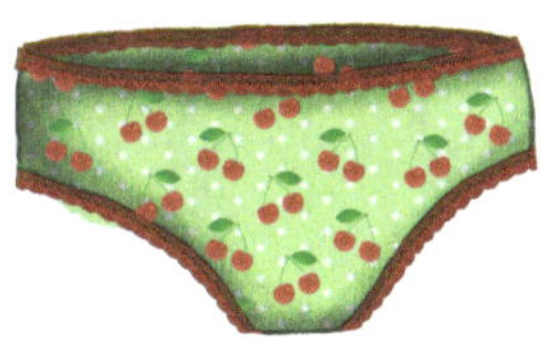

Not very early one morning, exactly six days after her 29$^{th}$ birthday, PSP woke up bleary eyed and heavy of head. She went through her morning ritual.

Am I in my own bed? Yes.

Am I injured? No.

Do I have my bag with my keys and credit cards in it? Yes, the contents spilling across the floor but everything was there.

As she turned on her side and glanced at the mess of discarded clothing on the floor she felt the beginnings of a feeling. It was a feeling of distress, of panic, of disbelief. Something was wrong, very wrong.

She rolled out of bed and onto the floor. She picked up her cute as a button meadow green skirt and laid it on the bed. She held the soft as an angel cream cardigan with embroidered leaping bunnies and pearl buttons against her cheek before laying that on the bed too. Her shoes were there, one lying forlornly on it's side in the doorway and the other half under and half outside the bed, their single demure straps still buckled. There, on a chair, in the corner of the room, was her palest pale lavender and cream lace bra, flung with abandon at the exact moment she fell towards the bed and instant deep, deep sleep.

She stood up and slowly turned three full circles around the room searching every nook and cranny, high and low. PSP ran to the front door, opened it, peered out to the left and to the right and shut it again firmly. As she walked up the hallway leading to her bedroom PSP realised that the unthinkable had happened. She had, indeed, lost her beautiful, pale blue with golden satin appliquéd stars, pants.

What was a girl to do?

PSP thought and she thought but she could not remember where she had left her treasured pants. The only thing to do was to re-visit every place she had been the previous night and find them.

MISSING!
HAVE YOU SEEN THESE FABULOUS PANTS?
REWARD

Ms JJ's
COCKTAIL LOUNGE

First she called Alfie and asked him to meet her at their usual haunt, a cute little bar not too far from home for either of them. Alfie was her best, cocktail-drinking, advice-giving, laugh-inducing friend. While he thought PSP was fabulous he had no designs on her fair body whatsoever. He was obsessed with the ever changing, buffed and chiseled waiters who were all waiting to be discovered and rushed to Hollywood. And the cocktails were excellent and the lighting flattering, as if they needed an excuse to go there.

"Alfie, Alfie I've lost my beautiful, beautiful, pants. Can you help?" PSP implored.

"Well, my dear, you had them very firmly in place when I left you, Alfie explained patiently. You gave me your trademark, I've-had-more-than-one-cocktail, skirt-in-the-air, flash, as I set off in pursuit of the gorgeous waitperson de jour. As you patted your skirt back into place you winked at me lecherously and said, "gonna see "what's up" with Alex." You know what you're like, adorable but unstoppable. So off you toddled.”

“Thanks love.” PSP perked up just a little. She had a little bit of hope and a delicious cocktail to sip upon. “Guess I'll go and see Alex then. Maybe I misplaced my beautiful pants in his dark, dank, den. Things could so easily go astray there.”

Alex was a darkly handsome gamer. How PSP even met him was unclear as he only ever left his game console for urgent supplies; energy drinks, beer and instant noodles. Since meeting PSP he also kept an emergency stash of cocktail supplies to lure her to him when she was at a loose end.

PSP knocked on Alex's door and waited. She knew from experience that he wouldn't answer the door until he finished playing whatever level he was currently on.

In the fullness of time he answered her knock and his surprise at seeing PSP again so soon was all over his face. Before he could get any kind of wrong ideas PSP explained she was only back to retrieve her beautiful lost pants. "So, where are they Alex? I need them now."

Alex looked a little confused. He often looked this way because in fact his mind was still in game land

and it took him a while to come back into the here and now.

"I don't think they're here but have a look around". So she did, picking up and folding assorted items of clothing strewn over the furniture and floor. She retrieved empty instant noodle containers and put them in the large black garbage bag in the corner of the room. She picked up discarded energy drink cans and beer bottles with just enough beer left to drown small inquisitive insects. When she finished the den was still dark, as Alex was adamant the curtains should never be opened, but it was tidy and completely bereft of sky blue and golden starred pants.

"I was really hoping they'd be here Alex. I don't know where else to look. Any ideas?" PSP implored.

"Apparently my cocktail selection was not to your taste last night even though you managed three before you ubered off. You went in search of a martini and according to you the best martinis are to be found in Liam's apartment"

"Oh. Well, I guess it's to Liam's I go then. See you Alex." And she gave him a friendly punch on the arm as he turned back to his game console."

Liam's apartment was all chrome and straight lines with accents in various shades of white. Surely a pair of pale blue and golden starred pants would not go unnoticed here?

PSP told Liam of her dilemma. She was so worried for the safety of her pants she didn't register Liam's lack of concern. Yes, she had indeed visited him last night. Yes, various items of clothing had been removed, Liam told her while blocking her way further into the apartment. "But to tell you the truth, this showing up at all hours is getting old. I turfed you out so I could get some sleep. Some of us have serious work to do. And as you can see there are no crazy slutty pants here. They'd spoil the aesthetic."

"Yes, sure, anaesthetic." PSP murmured distractedly as she ever so gently insinuated herself into the apartment. "You got anything to make a martini with Liam? I'm feeling quite unsettled".

"One martini and that's all!" And he led the way into the sparkling kitchen. "If it's any help you mentioned that long-haired, hand-me-down-clothing wearing, possibly flea-infested, person, Damian. I can't imagine you'd go running off after him but you were pretty crazy last night. You kept asking me if I could see you? Did I know who you were? You were shrill and embarrassing. Maybe it's time to get yourself some help girly. You're losing more than your pants."

Liam took PSP's now empty martini glass from her hand and placed it decisively in the shiny chrome dishwasher giving her no option but to leave.

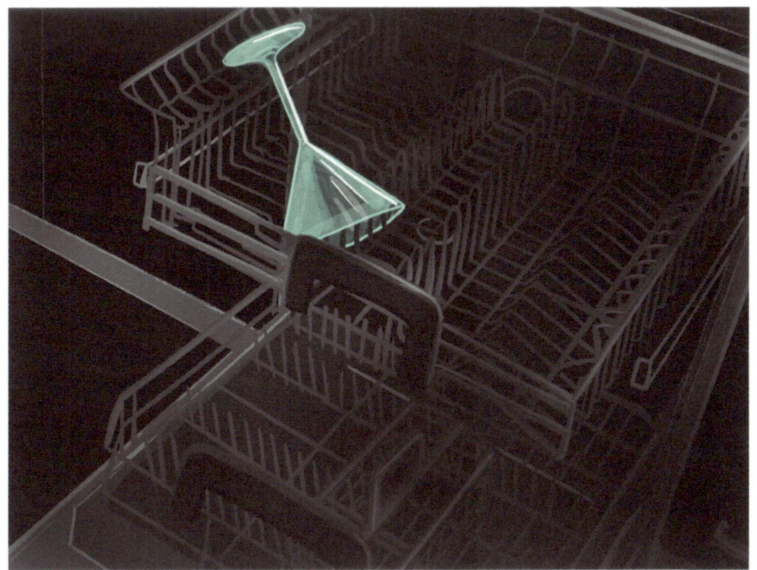

Damian. PSP caught her smiling self reflected in a shop window as she thought about going to see Damian. Must check all avenues thoroughly, she thought. He's a friend, not someone I'd loose my pants over she reasoned. And yes, she did remember, ever so vaguely, being in Damian's backyard with the wind-chimes and sculptures, fruits, flowers and vegetables taking up every bit of space in wild garden beds with no straight lines but were beautiful and soothing to look upon.

Damian greeted PSP with a broad smile, a big warm hug and a kiss on the tip of her nose. He led the way out to the two chairs in the garden where they had been the night before.

"What's wrong my sweet-pea? I can see you have something on your mind. Tell me all about it"

And so she did. Damian looked genuinely perplexed.

"No pants were left here my love although you did show them to me. They are exquisite."

PSP shook her head trying to make sense of everything. "So....I had my pants on when I left here......that's not possible......."

"You showed me pictures of your designs on your phone. Whether you were wearing pants or not I really couldn't say. I hope you find them. You're a gifted designer. My favourite is "let your lady garden run wild". Which one did you lose?"

"Stars in the morning" PSP sighed.

Damian could feel PSP's despair and moved closer to her "Oh no. Have you looked everywhere? What can I do to help?"

"I guess I'll go back and see Liam. Everything's so slippy-slidey shiny there maybe they slipped under something." PSP was losing hope of ever finding her beautiful pants again. But she had to try. "Can I come back here later and sit in the garden Damian? This has been a strange day."

"You're always welcome" And Damian lightly kissed the tip of her nose once more. "I'll have dinner ready

when you get back" Home grown veggies full of all
the good things."

Princess Slutty Pants; it was Liam who had first called her that. She thought it was hilarious at the time and it had stuck. But now there was a feeling tapping her on the shoulder and she would look at it as soon as she found her beautiful lost pants.

PSP knocked on Liam's door dreading the moment when he opened it and saw it was she, again. Things weren't as much fun with Liam as they once had been. Had he changed? Or had she? The door didn't open. She put her ear to it and listened. All she heard was....... nothing.

She fished around in her bag until she found the spare set of keys Liam had given her to be used "only in case of emergency". This was definitely one of those. She opened the door and quickly and quietly entered the apartment. She crouched down and looked under the bed with the white fluffy quilt covering it. No pants. She pulled the shiny cream bedside drawers away from the wall and looked behind them.

No pants. She looked under the magnolia couch. No pants. She lifted every ivory cushion. No pants. She checked behind the shiny chrome shelves. No pants.

PSP wanted another martini to dull her rising panic. Surely Liam wouldn't mind if she had just one more. She stood in the middle of the kitchen silently debating the issue with her self. Her eyes slid over the shiny surfaces. Nothing was out of place. Finally her eyes rested on the polished chrome rubbish bin in the corner. The little slidey door on the top was open. What was Liam thinking? She rushed to close it in case he blamed her for the oversight.

She stopped for a second as a thought bounced into her head. No, no, it was crazy, totally crazy but she did it anyway. PSP took the lid off the chrome rubbish receptacle in Liam's kitchen. She didn't have to look very far until she found the beautiful sky blue pants with gold appliquéd stars, tucked into an empty box of orange coloured fake cheese snacks.

FAKe
CHEEZe®
CHEESE
FLAVOURED
SNACK
100g

PSP shook the bedraggled pants to dislodge the vile orange powder and placed them tenderly in her handbag. She replaced the lid of the bin leaving the slidey door open. She dropped the "in case of emergency" keys on top and left the shiny, sharp-edged, everything-in-it's-place, apartment. Shutting the door firmly behind her with a "click".

And as she did so she listened to that feeling tapping on her shoulder and thought to her self "Princess Slutty Pants is NOT my name, thank you Liam. And I will do whatever I choose with my own beautiful pants".

PSP walked and walked and walked too numb to decide what to do next. She felt a little bit like crying, a little bit like laughing. She breathed in the cool night air and as she did she felt a calm wash over her. There, right in front of her, was Damian's wooden cottage with the colourful and bountiful garden.

PSP walked up the path and through the open front door following the welcoming glow and the ginger cat into the higgledy-piggledy kitchen. Damian smiled broadly and wrapped his arms around her. "Come and sit in the garden and tell me what happened sweet-pea"

As they sat side by side under the spreading branches of trees, flowers, vegetables and sleeping cats sprawled at their feet, PSP did indeed tell Damian her tale. They ate from a platter of roasted potatoes, capsicums, eggplants, pumpkin, zucchini and corn, each with just the right herbs and spices. And they sipped fresh apple juice that strangely tasted as good as any cocktail PSP had ever tasted.

When PSP finished talking and eating she just sat. She sat and that was enough. The warm summer breeze drifted around the two contented souls in the garden and as it did PSP smelled a smell she didn't recognise but it was so comforting, so warm and so delicious.

"What can I smell Damian?" I can't quite put my finger on it.....but it smells like love." PSP laughed thinking Damian would think her a very silly girl.

"That's my extra special summer pie. Raspberries, strawberries, blackberries and peaches in a light and buttery pastry and named after my favourite person in all the world......and yes, baked with love" Damian said looking PSP in the eyes with a look that said he didn't, not for one minute, think she was a silly girl. We'll eat it when it's cool so the ice-cream doesn't melt."

Princess Summer Pie leaned into Damian and kissed him right on his smiling, soft, kind mouth and knew that right here, right now, she had finally found everything she had ever wanted.

"Damian, I think I'm ready," she said, as she looked into his dark brown eyes. "I'm going to share my pants with the world. It's time." He smiled and nodded with understanding. "Oh, and I'll be staying here tonight if that's alright with you?" He answered with a kiss.

www.ingramcontent.com/pod-product-compliance
Lightning Source LLC
Chambersburg PA
CBHW041731300726
48981CB00005B/312